BETWEEN THEN AND NOW

WARDHAM BOOK 1

ZOE YORK

ZOYO PRESS

DEDICATION

this is something worth fighting for

For my in-laws, who will soon celebrate forty-five years of marriage

ABOUT THIS BOOK

Their story didn't start with a fairytale romance...
Romance is the last thing on Ian's mind. He's juggling the
family farm and a second job, his kids are a crazy handful
and every time he gets close to his wife, she snaps at him.
Their relationship started with a sizzling physical
connection, and he needs to find a way to leverage that into
reconnecting on a deeper level.

Their marriage wasn't chosen for love...
Carrie knows she's being too hard on her husband, but eight
years ago she had a one-night stand that turned into a
lifetime of diapers and dinners. She can't shake the feeling
that she wants more, or the fear that her husband won't
understand. **But they still chose each other...time and again.**

WELCOME TO WARDHAM

A sleepy village on the shores of Lake Erie, ready to explode with passion…

Part of the larger Lakeside Nights world!

Between Then and Now - Carrie & Ian Nixon (#1)

Their story didn't start with a fairytale romance. Their marriage wasn't chosen for love. But they still chose each other…time and again. *a novella*

What Once Was Perfect - Laney Calhoun & Kyle Nixon (#2)

He was her first love, and she's always owned a piece of his heart. *a novel*

Where Their Hearts Collide - Karen Miller & Paul Reynolds (#3)

When the girl next door meets the man of her dreams...at exactly the wrong time. *a novel*

When They Weren't Looking - Evie Calhoun & Liam McIntyre (#4)

She's not looking for love, he's not thinking about forever. It's not what they expected. But it might turn out to be just what they need. *a novel*

Beyond Love and Hate - Beth Stewart & Finn Howard (#5) *

First comes love, then comes marriage... Or maybe just a single night of passion, no strings attached. (Yeah, right!) *a novella*

No Time Like Forever - Chase Miller & Mari Beadie (#6)

It started with a kiss... *a novel*

Perfect No Matter What - Laney & Kyle Do Vegas (#7)

A business trip for Kyle and a last-minute rearranging of Laney's schedule provides the perfect fantasy escape to re-focus on what really matters. *a short story*

Beneath These Bright Stars - Evie & Liam's Wedding (#8)

It's time for Evie & Liam to say "I do". *a novella*

Forever Begins With a Kiss - Chase & Mari Get Hitched (#9)

Chase and Mari tie the knot in the middle of Mari's first big tour. *a novella*

All That They Desire - Evan West + Jessica Dornan + Brent Dornan (#10, coming soon)

Nothing about love is easy. *a novel*

————

* Finn Howard's brother, Ryan, lives in a town a few hours north of Wardham. If you like this series, you'll probably love Pine Harbour as well: small town military romance with heroes you'll fall in love with.

Pine Harbour

Love in a Small Town
Love in a Snow Storm
Love on a Spring Morning
Love on a Summer Night

READ LOVE IN A SMALL TOWN FOR FREE!

1

———

Ian Nixon had never before considered heading to the
pub instead of going home at the end of a work day. Eight
years of scrimping and saving, crying babies and tantruming
toddlers, medical troubles and family interference, and he'd
always embraced the drama.

But this wasn't something they could face together. Now
the drama was between them, and he didn't know if he could
handle another chilly conversation where he ended up the
bad guy when he had no clue what the problem was.

It had been a long, hot summer. Long days in the field.
Too many nights spent pouring over other people's book-
keeping. Carrie had been onboard with him picking up the
extra work, but maybe those nights would have been better
spent in their bed. Wrapped around his wife.

Had there been clues? Hindsight was a fucking bitch. Of
course there had been clues. A bite of the lip. An indrawn
breath. Wrinkled brows and shrugged shoulders. A few false

starts at conversations about work and balance, but the real alarms should have gone off when all of that faded.

Silence chilled like nothing else.

It took him a few weeks to notice, because he was an idiot. Then he got mad, which didn't help. Calling it out as passive aggressive crap really didn't go over well. Thinking that was the end of it was even worse.

But in between the empty smiles that didn't meet her eyes and the long-suffering sighs, happiness still flowed through and around his wife. She was at a great place with the kids. Drew had finally potty trained, and Kaylie was loving kindergarten. Her cake business was taking off, as it should, because Carrie turned sugar and butter and flour into something better than a slow fuck on a Sunday morning.

He swelled at the image of his curvy wife underneath him, kids somewhere far, far away. No, there was nothing better than a naked Carrie in the morning. But her German chocolate cake came pretty damn close.

Too bad he'd missed his opportunities to figure out what her problem was. There hadn't been any cake, or proper naked time, in far too long. His own fault.

Ian stopped at the end of his parents' lane. He'd been working their farm since he'd learned to walk, and until this summer, he'd never thought he'd walk away from it. But something had to give, and it sure as hell wasn't going to be his marriage. Whatever Carrie's problem was, they were going to sort it out. Together. Because if his wife was upset, he was upset.

He lifted his foot off the ground and gunned his bike for home.

———

"Daddy's going to be home any minute. Drew, get off the table. Kaylie, stop telling your brother what to do. You need to worry about yourself and let me be the mom, okay?" Carrie grabbed plates from the cupboard and set them on the counter. Cutlery. Cups of juice, glasses of water. "Drew? Would you rather milk or juice?"

"Mwilk, pwease."

The back door swung open, and Ian stepped into the kitchen. He shrugged off his leather jacket and hung it on a high hook. Good lord, he was handsome. Tired, though. When had he started to look so weary? Her heart ached to smooth that away, make it easier for him. Before she could say anything, Drew had leapt into his dad's arms, and just like that, Ian lit up. "Hey bud, were you a good boy today for Mommy?"

The three-year-old bobbed his head solemnly. "No time-outs, no twouble."

"That's what I like to hear. I'm gonna take a quick shower, you go play." Drew hit the ground running, and finally Ian was across the room. She lifted her face for a kiss. Too quick. Never enough time. She sighed, and he tipped her chin up with one knuckle. "Hey, babe."

"Hey."

"Missed you today. Miss you every day." That smile again. Too weak. What was on his mind?

"Everything okay?" He nodded and leaned in to dust her mouth with another kiss. "More," she whispered.

His tongued darted out and swiped at her bottom lip. Eight years and she still shivered. "I need to get cleaned up."

"Okay. Dinner's going to be ready in ten minutes. We gotta leave for hockey practice in half an hour." She didn't miss the wince. *Seriously?* "You forgot. Ian, come on...I put it in your calendar, but you have to look at the thing!"

He lifted his hands in surrender, but it didn't matter. Just like that, the mood shifted, and, since he must have felt it too, he turned and headed to their room. When had happiness become so fragile? How could she love her husband so much and still want to shake him silly?

They hadn't had enough time together this year. That was for sure. She knew why he was taking on more accounts, and it was good for their finances, but she'd offered to go back to work full-time instead. If they were out of the house at the same time, they'd have more time at home together. And not just the two of them—the kids missed their dad as well.

But each time they'd talked, he'd said the same thing. *Maybe next year. There's no rush.* Carrie knew his hope was that she'd get pregnant again, and it would stick this time. He didn't need to spell it out for her. *What's the point of starting a new job only to go on maternity leave again? And daycare for three is prohibitively expensive. Just do your cakes.*

Music swelled in the living room. Kaylie had managed to convince her brother to have a dance party. Two beautiful kids. Healthy and happy. That was enough. For her. Not for Ian.

They needed to talk about that. They needed to talk about a lot of things. She flipped off the oven. Not now, but maybe they could make some time.

She found Ian in the ensuite bathroom. He pulled off his t-shirt, and she paused for a moment in the doorway, letting her gaze drift lazily over his broad shoulders and long back.

He was a big guy, but moved with a casual grace that took her breath away. The smooth, hard muscles in front of her flexed as he swung his arms up over his head to stretch before unbuckling his belt and letting his jeans drop to the tile floor. Heat flooded her core as she realized he'd gone commando all day.

"Hey, again." She aimed for a sexy, cute tone, but it didn't hit the mark. He turned with a scowl. There was a time when this would be the moment he'd flash a wicked smile and invite her to join him in the shower. Now there wasn't a chance in hell they'd risk the kids discovering them naked together, and right now, she wasn't sure they liked each other enough to share such a small space. "I'm sorry for snapping."

"I'm sorry for forgetting."

She shrugged. Not the point of this conversation. "I was thinking, maybe we could ask your parents to babysit on Saturday night?"

"Sure. What do you want to do? Go to a movie?"

It was a reasonable suggestion, but her skin prickled with irritation. Before she could stop herself, her mind was snapping back a retort. *Time alone and you want to sit in a room full of strangers and not talk to each other?* "I was thinking something more...just the two of us. Maybe we could stay home."

"Why would we waste a babysitting opportunity?"

"There are things we can't do with the kids here." *One last shot to get it, buddy.* "Like, if they were at your parents, I could join you in the shower."

He grinned and stepped closer, sliding his hands around her waist. "Okay, we can ask my parents to babysit on the weekend so we can have shower sex."

She slapped at his back without effect as his whole body shook with silent laughter. "Ian! I'm serious."

"I get it, babe." He kissed her neck, squeezed her one last time, and moved back to the shower. "You want some quality time. We'll make that happen, I promise."

"That's not it—" Her protest died on her tongue as he stepped under the stream of water. It was more than just quality time, but how could she explain that to Ian when she couldn't properly quantify it for herself?

She was still grumpy when he walked back into their bedroom a few minutes later, wearing nothing but a towel. Beads of water rolled down his bulked up chest and clung to the rectangular patch of dark hair on his still flat abdomen. The shower might have been physically cleansing, but his shoulders still sagged under the weight of whatever was on his mind.

She knew what that felt like.

"Dinner ready?" His words were slow and careful, like he was trying hard not to piss her off. Like he needed to walk on eggshells around her. Damn.

She crossed the room and slid her arms around his waist, pressing her face against the damp, warm skin over his spine. "It's been a long year, eh?"

"Sure has."

"Did it all used to be easier?" Under her fingers, his abdominal muscles flexed, but he didn't respond right away. After a long silence, he took a deep breath and twisted to pull her around to his front.

"It was so long ago, babe, I don't know either of us can rightly say." He kissed her forehead. "I get that you want to talk, but we gotta have dinner and get to Kaylie's hockey game, right?"

She nodded numbly. Never enough time.

2

———

She fell asleep in Drew's room that night, and by the weekend, they'd both been making such an effort to be thoughtful and considerate that when the kids were dropped off at his parents, it seemed a shame to bring the mood down with a heavy talk, so they headed to Danny's to catch up with friends. Her closest friend, Karen Miller, was chatting at the bar with Evan West, who had been in Ian's grade in high school, so Carrie left the men to catch up for a minute and went in search of drinks. Karen joined her.

"Where's everyone else?"

Karen craned her neck to the back of the pub. "Ty is back there somewhere making out with his chickie of the week. Evie and Dale were here for a few minutes, but he threw a temper tantrum when Evan showed up, so they left."

There was no love lost between either woman and their friend's husband, whom they had long suspected was unfaithful. How anyone could cheat on Evie, who was funny and smart and drop-dead gorgeous, was beyond them. But

Dale also pushed their buttons by being extra possessive of his wife, particularly around her high-school boyfriend, Evan.

Which made no sense, because Evan was pretty openly gay.

But Dale was a douche, and logic wasn't a factor.

Besides, despite having a good week, she really wasn't one to judge other relationships when her own might be in a precarious position itself.

Before long, the table had filled, and when Ian caught up, he pulled a chair up right behind her and leaned forward, sharing her space. His breath was hot and distracting on the side of her neck, and though he seemed to be paying attention to the conversation, his fingers were busy in the wavy tangle of hair cascading from her low ponytail.

It had been too long since she'd had his attention like this. She eased her hands backward through the slats of her chair and reached for his legs, reciprocating the gentle touch. Before long, he'd lifted all of her hair into a twisted bun, and his fingers were resting on bare skin at the top of her spine.

Prickly awareness coursed down and out from that hot contact, and she was halfway to proposing they sneak off to the restrooms when he shifted his hand sideways and squeezed her neck, holding the possessive position for a few beats before bringing his lips to the curve of her ear. "Let's get out of here, angel."

They quickly made their goodbyes, and a quiet thrill danced through her heart that Ian held her close until they got back to their SUV, where he held her even closer and pressed home a kiss that promised more to come at the end of their short drive.

Ian drove, and she was grateful for the automatic transmission that allowed their fingers to remain tangled even as Ian nudged the vehicle into drive. The silence was comfortable and warm, and she was torn on breaking it with chatter, but information needed to be shared.

"Karen said that Evie and Dale left before we got there. They were fighting."

"Guy's a douche." Good that they were in agreement on that point. "Too bad they've got kids caught in the middle of that."

"Yeah."

"Is she going to need anything?"

"You think they're going to break up?"

"Writing's on the wall there. Just a matter of time." Ouch. He wasn't wrong, but it hurt her heart to hear the words said out loud.

"I don't know. Her mom will probably step up. Might be good for her." Evie's father had passed away the previous year, and the loss of her life partner had impacted hard on Claire Calhoun. "Maybe they won't break up."

"Babe, some people aren't meant for forever." He lifted her hand to his mouth. "Some guys don't know what they have."

His words tugged the corners of her mouth north again. "Oh?"

"I know what I've got. I don't always show it, but I'm lucky to be your husband, Carrie Nixon."

"Best mistake ever?" She meant the words to land lightly. It was a standing joke between them, but all that had gone unsaid between them over the last few months weighed the words down on her tongue, and her voice cracked.

"Don't do this, not tonight." His features pinched together. He didn't let go of her hand, but the easy softness in his grip faded, replaced with a subtle tension that told her it was an effort to keep touching her.

"I'm not doing anything," she whispered. Tears threatened, hot bubbles at the edge of her vision.

"You're dragging old shit into a new argument. Shit I didn't even know was in your head. An argument I didn't even know we were having."

"We're not!" Were they? Was it all one big fight that just ebbed like the tide? "I don't know why I said that."

He didn't answer. He didn't need to. She tentatively lifted her gaze to read his expression, but he didn't look over at her, instead keeping his eyes on the road ahead. A muscle twitched along his jaw, and she squeezed his hand, willing him to turn and see her. See that she wasn't mad. That she was just scared and strangely alone and not dealing with that well.

"I don't think we were a mistake."

"Damn straight."

"But we weren't in love when we got married, Ian. That's never going to be something I forget."

"Never asked you to."

"We just can't talk about it."

"We can talk about it, babe. But you can't yell at me about it."

"I didn't yell."

"You cried. That's worse."

"Didn't cry. No tears."

"Sad voice, choked up...sounded like crying. Carrie, that kills me, you know?" He dragged a deep breath into his lungs.

"I just wanted an evening without a fight. Come on, let's go in."

With a start, she realized they were home. "Wait—" She unbuckled her seat belt and reached across the center console. "Slide your seat back."

"Carrie, I'm not—"

"Give me a chance to get the mood back, please?" She was grateful she'd worn a skirt tonight. "Scoot back, and close your eyes." He still hadn't moved, but at least he wasn't getting out of the truck. "I want to show you what I've got on under this skirt."

Thank god for his healthy libido. A lecherous grin spread across his face as he flicked his gaze to her hemline. "Please tell me the answer is nothing." She waited for his gaze to hit hers again before offering a slow nod. His already smoldering interest caught a burst of oxygen from her answer, and while he slid his seat back with his left hand, his right arm was hauling her into his lap. "We gotta stop fighting, babe."

"We weren't fighting," she whispered.

"We were doing something," he muttered as he arranged her thighs on either side of his, his thumbs pressing hard into soft flesh. "And it wasn't this."

"This isn't everything."

"No, but it's something. Evie and Dale, they don't have this. They should, because she's sweet and hot."

"You think Evie's hot?" This teasing was truly light-hearted. She'd never doubted Ian's attraction to her, not even during and after her pregnancies. She'd gained an extra ten pounds with each kid that was never going away, and she hadn't been skinny when they met. How much she bitched, now that seemed to have an impact, but thankfully it had a short half-life.

"Babe, you think Evie's hot. I'm just stating objective facts. She's a ten, and Dale's not, so he's an idiot. But I don't want to talk about them anymore. I want to talk about..." He let the sentence drop off as his fingers disappeared into the shadow between their bodies. She sucked in a wavering breath as he curled first one and then two digits into her wet heat. "All right?"

She nodded.

"Fuck, I'm a lucky man."

"Mmmm. Right now, I feel like the lucky one." Thank god for private country properties. They didn't have a farm, but they were outside of town, and their driveway curved around to a garage at the back of their house. Without a second thought, she peeled her t-shirt off in what she hoped was a sexy move. It sure felt sexy. She was hyper-aware of his breath on her chest and wanted more of that. She arched her back, riding his fingers with slow and deliberate intent, taking her own pleasure but doing so in a way that she could feel was working on him as well. His other hand stroked from her ass to her back, a hot slide toward her bra that resulted in a quick release.

"You've gotten good at that over the years."

"Gotta be quick with the rugrats always threatening to interrupt." He pressed her back, laying her upper body against the steering wheel. "Don't need to be quick tonight, though."

There shouldn't be anything sexy about two grownups squeezed into the driver's side of an SUV in their own driveway, their empty and comfortable house a few feet away, but at that moment, nothing was hotter than Ian perusing her body spread out in front of him. He twisted his hand, still pumping slowly in and out of her sex, and rested his thumb on her clit. She watched him through hooded eyes as delicious sensations washed over her body. He wasn't building her toward an orgasm so much as shifting her into an altered state of arousal. "Don't play with me," she panted. "Make me—"

He pulled his fingers out of her pussy and tapped them on the inside of her thigh. "You don't want me to play with you?" His other hand stilled on her breast, abandoning its path to her nipple.

She thrust her hips, helplessly, because there wasn't much room to move, and with her legs folded underneath her, she had no leverage. "That's not what I meant. Ian!" He chuckled, and she slid her own hand between her thighs. His laughter faded as she touched herself, and he licked his lips.

"Keep doing that." He loosened his belt, then lifted his hips the barest amount, just enough to give him some play with his jeans.

Sex in the car. What were they thinking? They weren't, for the first time in weeks, maybe longer, and it was glorious.

No, what was glorious was his wife perched on his lap, back arched like a pinup girl, topless, with her short skirt pushed up around her lush, pale hips.

The details of what she was doing with her hand were lost in the night shadows, but he could still feel her slippery excitement under his fingers, and couldn't wait to replace her hand with his cock. The full moon lit up her bare shoulder and highlighted the twist of her arm as she languidly stroked her pussy. His gaze shifted to the swell of her right breast, and the thought of getting his mouth on her nipple caused his erection to pulse painfully against the damn zipper, as if reminding him that he was doing a piss-poor job of freeing the dirty bastard. Didn't he know it.

With an expletive studded rip, he had his jeans open and his cock in his hand. Wouldn't care if the pants were damaged, either. "Come here, babe."

He cupped the back of her neck and pulled her to him. Her lips parted, an invitation he'd take. His biceps flexed as he closed the gap between them, and he wanted to roar. Fuck, yes. This was what it was all about. There was too much fucking noise between them most of the time. Carrie on top of him, all soft and wet and willing, this was what they needed to hang on to. Needed to make more time for.

As she sank into the kiss, her weight shifted onto his torso and his hand got pinned between their bellies. His hand, and his cock. He reacted instinctively to the gentle squeeze and jerked his hips, his balls connecting with her damp heat. *Oh, fuck.*

All thoughts of going slow and taking their time were vanquished by that contact. He needed to be inside her. As if reading his mind, she pressed up on his shoulders, lifting her hips enough to re-align their cores. She was more than ready for him, but he used the thinking part of his brain and paused.

"Babe." Both of them were breathing loudly, or their breath was loud because it was otherwise quiet, he wasn't sure. But she wasn't listening to him, she was kissing his jaw and panting, wriggling around on the top of his cock. "Babe. Stop. Do we need a condom?"

"Oh…" She scrunched up her face. "No. It's an okay time. I just want you inside me."

"You and me both. You sure?"

"Just for a minute." She wriggled out of his grasp and sank onto him, eliciting matching groans. Nothing between them was pure heaven, even if it meant pulling out. Or not, but that was Carrie's call. He'd happily make babies with her until they weren't physically able, but it wasn't his body that bore them, or lost them. His heart, but maybe not as much as hers.

He spread his fingers wide around her hips, his thumbs notched over the top of her thighs. He loved the feel of her muscles flexing with need under his hands, her body the perfect combination of soft and strong. Sweet and fierce, that was his wife. He pulled them together, then held her there, enjoying her helpless wiggles as she tried to work her clit against the base of his cock.

"Slow down," he murmured. "Do too much more of that, and I'm going to fill you up."

She gasped against his mouth, and even in the shadows he knew that turned her on. They needed to have a conversation about birth control, and maybe not while they were in the middle of fucking.

He twisted his hands into her hair, finding the elastic that he'd wound her ponytail around earlier. Eight years of wanting to see her undone meant he knew his way around hair accessories, and with a flick of his fingers, the elastic shot across the car and her bright red locks tumbled around her shoulders.

"I fucking love your hair, babe." His words were backed up by his cock twitching inside her, and she surged in response, starting a slow ride that he could get on board with. He squeezed her hips and helped her find a rhythm that soon had them both groaning. He loved that she still dyed her hair bright colours. The red was by far his favourite. The night they'd met, it had been freshly coloured, and she'd worn it in pigtails. He hadn't been able to stop looking at her at all night, wondering if he'd ever have a chance with a woman like her.

Even after they started dating, he'd known that she had big plans. Plans that couldn't include a country boy, tied to a family farm.

And then he'd gone and knocked her up. He'd lived with that guilt for eight years, and probably would for the rest of his life. Carrie's grand adventure had gotten her as far as baking the occasional birthday and wedding cake in a modest ranch house on ten acres carved out of a sugar bush. He wanted more for her than that. He wanted to give her the world.

"Iannnnn," she groaned, her face pressed into the side of his head, her arms wrapped around his neck. He felt it too, an urgency to her rise and fall as she tightened around him, and he sucked in a breath, willing himself to hold off until she'd taken all the pleasure she could. He let her go, and she bounced faster and harder on his lap as he turned his focus to her soft, creamy breasts, full and supple in his hands as he cupped them, teasing one nipple with his thumb as he sought the other with his mouth.

Her nipples were flat, even after nursing two children, but the pillowy tissue popped out at his gentle urging, and her pussy clenched around him as he licked and sucked first one, and then the other, to a sensitive point. Carrie had always liked nipple play—when they met, she'd had them pierced, thin gold hoops that she'd beg him to tug on just before she came. The rings were long gone, but he could still help her over the edge with a scrape of his thumbnail and a nip of teeth.

With a final surge up, and down again, she stilled in his lap, trembling inside and out. He slicked his hands down her sweat drenched sides and around to her back, holding her against his body as she went limp, overwhelmed by her orgasm. He was on the edge himself, and he wanted nothing more than to start driving hard into her swollen core, to spill himself inside her...fuck, even thinking about it was a threat to his control.

But they had all night. They weren't teenagers, and the car wasn't their only option.

"That was hot." He tugged gently on her hair, tilting her face toward his so he could swipe a lazy kiss across her lips. "Let's go inside."

She flexed her pussy around him. "What about you?"

He chuckled. "I'm not done with you, babe. I want you stretched out on our bed."

She whimpered, but her smile told him she was pleased.

He pushed the truck door open, and Carrie eased away from his body, shivering at the temperature drop. He grabbed her t-shirt and slid it over her naked breasts, then took a minute to tuck himself back into his jeans before they climbed out. He pulled her hard against his body once they were standing on the ground, and they walked inside as one, where he pulled her into the shower and warmed her up, first with a gentle wash cloth and then his mouth. When it was his turn again, she led him to their bed and rode him long and slow and hard, until he lifted her off, coming hard between their bodies, and they needed the wash cloth again.

3

Things between them were better, but a week of good sex and early evenings hadn't miraculously solved the underlying issues in their marriage.

Carrie had broached the subject when he got back from morning chores. "And then you say or do something little, and I lose my mind. I shouldn't, but I do, and I worry that means—"

"We're just fine." He closed the gap between them, mindful that the kids would be up any minute. "You've been 'Mom' for a long time. You have a hard time turning it off."

"I don't mother you." She stiffened against his chest.

"Little bit." He cupped her chin, her face small in his hand, and she closed her eyes. He loved the softness of her skin under his calloused fingers. A sigh escaped her lips, and he knew it wasn't enough, but it was something. And little bits of something that they could piece together was all that they had. Between parenting and work, they were running flat out, especially with making positive time for each other.

Neither of them wanted to fight at night. Or in the morning. So when talking headed in that direction, they were both all too eager to shift to what they did best. But sex wasn't the answer.

He was committed to getting them back on track, and hoped that after tonight, there wouldn't be any more secrets between them. He'd thought about coming clean after talking to Evan at the pub, but then she'd gone on about Evie and Dale, and he wanted to reassure her that they weren't the same. Reassure himself too, if he was being honest.

He looked at his phone again, for what felt like the twentieth time that day, and it was only eight in the morning.

"Waiting for a call?" He started at the male voice behind him and turned to see his younger brother leaning against the kitchen counter. "I saw Carrie leaving with the kids, she said to let myself in and grab a cup of coffee."

"Hey. Yeah, help yourself." He gestured at the pot.

"You're distracted."

Ian shrugged. "What are you doing here before school?"

"I need to borrow your chop saw, going to lay some flooring tonight." Kyle had recently bought an old schoolhouse, just outside of town, and was renovating it himself. He'd put up with a fair number of jokes about it being a fitting abode for an elementary school teacher, but Ian had to admit, it was the perfect bachelor pad. And Kyle was a committed bachelor, swearing off love after two disastrous relationships.

"You need help?"

"Nah. Evan's in town, and he'll probably convince Ty to come along too." The West brothers were as opposite as night and day, but they worked well together—so well, in fact, that they'd gone into business together, starting a fledgling winery and, more recently, starting to invest in downtown Wardham real estate. Ian wasn't as close to them as his brother was, but he had a lot of respect for the Wests.

"The saw's in the garage, hang on." He stepped through the adjoining door from the kitchen into the clutter of his garage. There was just enough room to park his bike there. Carrie's SUV lived outside.

Kyle followed him, whistling when he got to the door.

"Shut up."

"You got a big project here, man. Gonna make the little lady park outside all winter?"

"First of all, don't call her that." Ian grabbed the big saw, made sure the safety latch was on, and thumped it into his brother's chest. "Second of all, I've got more important things to worry about."

"Nothing's more important than your woman."

"What would you know about that?"

Kyle's jaw tightened at that, but instead of answering, he stepped back to the kitchen and set the saw down on the floor.

"So, I talked to Evan." Ah. The real reason for the visit. "You know what you're doing?"

"Yep."

"If I could just give you some advice—"

"I don't want, or need, your advice."

"Carrie's going to be pissed."

"You let me worry about Carrie."

"Are you?"

Ian crossed his arms over his chest. He was the big brother in every way, taller, older and his job was more physical, so he probably had ten extra pounds of muscle on Kyle, but he didn't relish the thought of pounding his brother into the ground. Much. "I don't see how that's your business."

"She's like my sister. And she's had a rough year."

"How would you know that?"

"I see her, at Mom and Dad's, around town. Always has the kids with her, juggling a cake or groceries. You've been absent, man."

"I've been working, Kyle."

"Is that what she wants?"

"It's what we need."

"Are you in financial trouble?"

God, no. He didn't want Carrie to ever experience the poverty of her childhood again. "We're fine. I'm just building up a cushion, paying down the mortgage. Trying to get ahead."

"Don't be a hero. Talk to Carrie. Maybe she doesn't understand."

Maybe Kyle didn't understand how this wasn't any of his business. "Got it."

"Don't shoot the messenger."

"I said—Hey, you know who we haven't talked about in a while?"

"Okay, point made."

"No, I don't think it was. What happened last year after the funeral?" Kyle didn't need to answer that. He'd gone on a bender and broken up with his live-in girlfriend after seeing Laney Calhoun at her father's funeral. Kyle and Evie's sister had dated in college, and his brother never did get over that breakup. "Where is she now, still in Calgary?"

"Chicago." Kyle picked up the saw he'd come for and moved to the back door.

"Five hour drive, less in the middle of the night. You ever think about just getting in your truck?"

This was deeper and meaner than their conversations usually went. Ever, really. But Kyle had picked at his scab—Ian was just returning the favour.

His brother scrubbed a hand across his jaw. "All the time, man. All the fucking time."

"What's stopping you?"

"I can't bear the thought of hurting her again."

"Who says you'd hurt her?"

"We're not you and Carrie, okay? There's no happy ever after for me and Laney. Everyone around here needs to get that straight."

———

PRESCHOOL DAYS WERE THE BEST. There was something about being temporarily childfree that increased her productivity by five-hundred percent. After dropping Kaylie at school and Drew at the half-day program in the Presbyterian church basement, Carrie cut back across downtown Wardham for the main road to Essex, the larger town near the freeway.

She'd come to love their sleepy little village, but downtown had seen better days. Not for the first time, Carrie mused on how a few small changes would make a big difference. There had been a few attempts to bring tourist dollars to town, but they'd been focused on nostalgia—Wardham needed to move into the 21st century. The outdoor hockey tournament was a great draw, but a modern, attractive arena would be a good blizzard backup. Of course, that wasn't an original idea, and the town council and small business association had been at odds over the investment for years. If she was a local business person, she'd...

She'd what? Carrie sighed to herself. Her imagination could run off with a dozen ideas of fun businesses she'd start up. She'd thought about talking to the West brothers more than once but always chickened out. No, not chickened out. Wised up to reality. She had enough on her plate as it was, she didn't need to start something new. And really, where would she even start?

She needed to appreciate the good life that she had. She'd come a long way from the little apartment over the laundromat on Wyandotte Street, saving all her pennies.

Ha. So what if she hadn't gone to England. Here she was, driving to Essex, and if the shops there didn't have what she needed, she'd head to Windsor next. Not quite the same thing. The countryside between the towns was lovely enough, but she imagined the British communities were much more picturesque. Not that Carrie would ever know. At one time, she planned to backpack through Europe. She'd been working at a country & western bar in Windsor, hustling hard for tips from drunk wannabe cowboys, when she met Ian.

That night changed everything.

He wasn't wearing the hat or boots, but he had the swagger, and he could dance better than most. He stayed to last call, and she surprised both of them by inviting him back to her apartment. He gave a sober buddy his keys and told him to come back for him in the morning.

He'd been cute. More than cute. She hadn't been able to

stop watching him, and she caught his eye enough that she knew the feeling was mutual.

If she'd had any doubts he was a real deal country boy, they disappeared when he unabashedly stripped down to nothing—the sun had kissed his arms to mid-bicep, although his torso wasn't without a faint tan. She'd thought lazily that maybe he had a pond. She'd like to go skinny dipping with him. Leap onto his back and wrap her legs around his lean hips. Hold on to his broad shoulders and press her naked breasts into his back and drift into the cool water together.

As he opened his button-fly jeans, revealing snug briefs underneath, she'd whispered for him to stop. He was hard and sinewy in all the right places, with shadows and valleys she wanted to explore with her mouth and hands and eyes, but her touch first went to the line where dark faded to light on his arm, neatly following the curve of his muscles. "Nice farmer's tan."

He read the husky tone in her voice correctly, not taking offense at all, and he reached for the button on her jeans, using it to leverage her closer. "Let's see yours." He hovered his mouth above hers. "I bet it leads me straight to heaven."

It was a total line, and it totally worked. She whimpered into his kiss, and the next thing she knew, they were rolling around naked on her bed, taking turns pinning each other down and tracing all the tan lines they could find. That led to playing connect the dots on the four moles on her tummy, and guessing the story behind each of his seven scars. It was the best and strangest hook up she'd ever had.

When he finally donned a condom and slid inside her, she welcomed him with wild abandon. The first time was hard and fast. The second took longer, and sparked something sweet and scary, and they fell asleep wrapped around each other.

Carrie blinked at the memory. She was almost in Essex. She'd forgotten that they'd slept entwined like that from the very first night. For the longest time, the dominant memory was of waking up in the middle of the night and feeling Ian harden between her legs.

"You're awake."

"So are you." She swirled her hips, teasing his length along her slick sex.

"Do you want to…" He groaned as she reached the tip of him. "I should grab a condom."

He should have. But she was sore, and stupid, and didn't want to fuck. She just wanted to play and then brazenly ask for his mouth.

How different their lives would be if he hadn't come between her legs. If she hadn't had to tell him a month later, on their fourth date, that she was pregnant, and there was no doubt it was his.

She hadn't even wanted to date him, not really. He was cute, and when he was looking at her, she felt it in a tingly way down to her very core. But they were too different, and she just didn't see them getting serious.

That was a secret she'd take to her grave, because when she lost the baby two weeks after their courthouse wedding, he'd held her. When she found out. In the shower. In their bed, which was so newly theirs she still thought of it as hers. In the shower again, as she sobbed at the blood swirling down the drain. He hadn't known what to say, but somehow had known exactly what to do, and in doing so, everything that had been hers became theirs. A few months later, in an uncharacteristic moment of emotional vulnerability, Ian asked her if she wanted a divorce. She'd been able to honestly tell him that she didn't. That she wanted a future. Wanted his children.

She'd taken him to bed, and Kaylie was conceived.

She shivered. It would be a different thing, now, if she ended up pregnant again. She'd find love in her heart for a third child. Put off her secret dream of opening a bakery or bed and breakfast. It would be okay.

But it wasn't a coincidence that she was rehashing the beginning of their relationship this week. Their little oops—are unprotected sex mistakes ever little?—had been on her mind. Ian would be thrilled. Another secret she'd have to keep.

Carrie shook her head. It was probably going to be a non-issue. It hadn't been the right time in her cycle, and she knew her body a lot better now than she had eight years previously. But she'd still be relieved when her period arrived. But right now, she had cake supplies to buy. The shop in Essex offered a discount for cash purchases, for reasons she'd rather not think too hard about, so she pulled into the drive-thru teller machine at the Essex branch of their bank and withdrew enough money for her shopping and incidentals for the rest of the week. Ian liked to do a cash budget at the beginning of the month, but he also left enough money in their joint chequing account to avoid bank charges, and just in case of extra shopping, like this trip for a last minute cake request for one of the preschool teachers.

She almost didn't look at the receipt when it spit out of the machine. Almost crumpled it up and tucked it into the provided slot for recycling.

Instead, she grabbed it and tossed it onto the passenger seat, where it slipped under her purse. So it wasn't until she parked in front of Mary's Cakes and More baking supply store that the numbers on the slip caught her attention.

The lack of numbers, that was.

With the three hundred dollars she'd just taken from their account, there was less than fifty dollars left.

Cold fear slithered down her face and across her chest. It didn't make any sense. She reached for her phone to call Ian.

Ian.

When was the last time she'd looked at the bank balance? A few weeks earlier, probably. She hadn't told him she'd be taking money out today. She usually used her cake money envelope for these trips. They were usually budgeted for.

Usually.

Where was all their money? She blinked hard, straining to remember what the balance usually was. At least three thousand dollars, to avoid monthly bank charges. And a bit more for incidental spending. She looked down at the phone in her hand. She should call him. Or the bank.

Yes. She'd call the bank. Her hands shook as she flipped over the bank card and dialed the toll-free number on the back. Tapped in her card number and access code. Listened to Muzak. Her hands were still shaking when a guy who called himself Ryan greeted her by name, and when she responded, she realized that her voice was shaking too. Fantastic.

Ryan assured her that there hadn't been any suspicious activity on the account and asked if she'd talked to the other person on the account. No. Ryan didn't ask her why. She asked that of herself, afraid to hear the answer. Herself didn't say anything, still numb with shock. Probably for the best.

She darted into Mary's, and came out with what she needed. She was vaguely aware of paying at the till and being pleasant, enquiring about the time, and begging off a long chat about the latest trends in icing colours because she had to pick up Drew from preschool.

The drive home wasn't filled with memories like the drive in. This time, raw emotion, too big to be named, flooded her being and spilled into the truck around her.

There was a good explanation. Of course there would be. She just needed to call him and ask. *Why did you secretly drain our accounts today, honey?*

She couldn't call him if that was how the question would come out.

If she waited until he got home, she probably wouldn't need to formulate a question. He didn't always address it, but he knew when she was upset. Would he know that this time talking wasn't optional? Maybe she should go and find him.

After picking up Drew, she headed home, but instead of turning into their driveway, she kept going.

"Mama missed it! The house! Mama!"

She shot Drew a tremulous smile in the rearview mirror. "I know, baby. I'm taking you to Grandma's house instead, okay?"

Drew chattered about cookies and saying hi to cows as they travelled the three concession blocks to the farm. She braced herself to be circumspect if Ian's bike was parked beside the house, but it wasn't. *Where was he?*

Eleanor Nixon was hanging laundry on the line, and

Drew raced to help her. Carrie took a deep breath and slowly followed. "Hey, Ellie."

"Carrie! This is a pleasant surprise. Ian's gone into town to pick up a new drill bit. They've broken three already this morning."

"What are they doing?"

"Some sort of make-work project in the implement shed while they wait for the fields to dry out." Her mother-in-law shrugged. "Do you want to come in for tea?"

Two cookies and a cup of tea later, Carrie was feeling both better and silly at the same time. There would be a reasonable explanation, and she didn't need to interrupt Ian's work day to get it. She stood, ready to say goodbye, when Eleanor waved her over to the computer in the corner of the living room.

"Come and look at the custom labels I found online for Kaylie's school supplies."

Carrie grinned. Eleanor's credit card was getting a workout since she'd discovered online shopping. "A sharpie and fabric tape has worked just fine so far, Ellie."

"But these have ballerinas! Or fairies." Eleanor misread the look on Carrie's face. "Or firetrucks, if you want to be gender neutral."

"It's not—"

"Humour me, Carrie."

"Okay. Let me just call Ian and tell him we stopped by, but we're going home." Carrie pulled her cell phone out of her bag. "Darn. My battery died, I'll just use the house phone."

"Dial-up, sweetie. Use my cell." How Eleanor managed to function online with just a dial-up connection, Carrie couldn't understand. She spied her mother-in-law's phone on the kitchen counter and headed to the other room to grab it.

Drew bumped into her as he shot like a missile to investigate the pretty pictures his grandmother was looking at. "Dwagons, Gramma?"

"Sure thing, sweetpea." The patter of dragon talk faded as Carrie pushed her way out on to the sun porch. She punched Ian's number into the phone and held it up to her ear.

He picked up after three rings but didn't say anything right away. She could hear muted conversation in the background, then Ian quickly said, "Hang on, Mom."

"No, Ian, it's—" But he was gone again, resuming his muffled conversation, like he was holding the phone to his shirt.

"Sorry about that. I'll be back soon, okay? I just...nothing. Listen, before I forget, I'm going to tell Carrie that I'm working late tonight, and I need you to back me up on that, okay?"

What?

"Mom?" A bell chimed in the background, like Ian had walked through a door. "Hello?"

Her husband thought he had a dropped signal. Her husband. Who was going to lie to her.

*Maybe there's a good reason...*Twice in one day? What the hell was going on?

"Ian?"

"Fuck. Carrie. What..." He let out a heavy exhale.

She waited for him to say something, anything. He didn't.

"Nevermind." The word squeezed out, compressed by fear and adrenaline. She let the phone tumble to the bench beside her, her hands too heavy to hold on.

From the living room, Drew's shriek of delight stabbed through her haze of confusion, and she headed back inside, willing herself to hold it together long enough to ask her mother-in-law if she could pick Kaylie up from school and watch the kids through dinner.

Eleanor wrinkled her brow, trying to figure out what had changed in the last two minutes.

Everything. Maybe.

Carrie kissed Drew on the forehead and made it to her SUV before the tears started to flow.

4

———

She barely had enough time to find a box of tissues before his bootsteps pounded across the back deck. Her heart squeezed. She wasn't ready for this, whatever it was going to be. But then the screen door slapped against the siding, heavy steps moved across the kitchen, and she didn't have a choice.

"Carrie!" His voice carried enough urgency that she felt a flicker of hope. "Where are you?"

Not enough hope to answer, but it was something. She sat perfectly still, cross-legged in the middle of their bed. Where Drew had been conceived and borne. Where they'd just started reconnecting. A wave of uncontrollable emotion rocked through her. She knew she wasn't thinking clearly, and it couldn't be stopped.

He loomed large in the doorway, his chest lifting and flexing as he breathed—maybe in exertion, maybe in an effort to calm down. His expression was unreadable, and fear climbed back to the top of the hierarchy of her emotions.

He repeated her name, this time as a question, although she had no idea what the answer might be. "Babe, what you heard...I don't know why you're reacting like this, but you've got it all wrong."

"What do I have all wrong?" Her words tumbled out in a whisper.

He scrubbed a hand over his face and rocked back on his heels. Instead of answering, he narrowed his eyes, like he was trying to guess what was in her head. "Do you trust me?"

No. The answer was swift and harsh, even though she didn't voice it. She didn't need to, he saw it on her face, and swore under his breath.

"Well, that's a problem." He propped his hands on his hips and hung his head. A long silence stretched between them, her racing, pounding heartbeat a painful metronome, counting off each lost beat. All the unspoken words. "Carrie..." He lifted his head up. "What's going on?"

"I don't know." It wasn't much, but it was the truth.

"I'm sorry about tonight. It's not what you think."

"I don't think..." she trailed off, not wanting to even say the words. "I know you would never cheat on me."

"Then what's with the freakout? I called my mom back, and she said you took off like a bat out of hell."

Carrie winced. "Sorry."

"Don't be sorry. Just tell me what's going on."

"Did you..." She trailed off, willing herself to find exactly the right words. This was a conversation too important to fuck up. *Don't make any assumptions, just be objective.* "I went to the bank this morning," she whispered.

"What?" He pulled up slightly, and she flinched at the recoil, but he looked more confused than defensive. "Why?"

"Not the...I mean, the bank machine. I took cash out and saw the...there's no money in our account, Ian."

Confusion faded to horror as comprehension dawned on his face. "And then you called me."

She nodded.

"I move money around all the time, Carrie."

"Never from our chequing account. Always savings. And you tell me. You might not think I'm listening, but I am. You didn't tell me about this. And it wasn't planned, or you would have just used our savings account."

He shifted in discomfort, and a heavy ache settled in her chest.

"What are you hiding from me, Ian?"

He stepped back, swinging his arms out to his side seemingly without purpose. He turned a half circle, then twisted back toward her and stared. Obvious frustration rolled off him in waves so tangible she would be surprised if she couldn't reach out and touch it. He held her gaze, his own hard and dark, then dropped to one knee and undid his boot laces. His eye contact didn't break, even as he switched legs, and then he was up and kicking off his boots as he strode toward the bed.

She held up her hands to stop him, but he pulled up just short. He held her gaze and began to speak. "I don't want to tell you right now. I want you to trust me." His words came out slowly, as if he was choosing them with care. "You are my wife. Whom I fucking adore. And you don't trust me. So we've got a big problem, and we're going to sort that out first."

He leaned into her personal space and bracketed his hands on the bed on either side of her knees. His arms were long, but not long enough that he could do this without being right on top of her. "I promise you, babe, that I will tell you everything. But any secrets I've been keeping have been out there, about stuff and things and nonsense. And right now, I'm looking at you, and you're wound up tighter than a straw bale at dusk, so I gotta think, maybe there are some secrets that you've been keeping."

Her breath caught shallow in her throat, and his eyes warmed as hers widened.

"Awww, babe. Carrie, my angel..." He shifted his weight to one arm, and cupped her face with his other hand. "What have you got going on in your head?"

"Nothing," she breathed.

"Liar."

"I'm not." She heard the denial spill out of her mouth and wanted to take it back. Wanted to replace it with everything that had been locked in her head for far too long. But sharing would be ugly, and Ian wouldn't understand. He'd want to, he'd try, but at some point, hearing all of her doubts and ancient thoughts would offend him, and they'd be fighting again, only with a lot more ammunition.

"So you won't trust me with that, either."

"I want to."

"But..."

"I don't know where to start." *Or how much to share.*

As if he could read her mind, his nostrils flared, and he let out a huff of air. "Don't pick and choose, Carrie. That's what leads to messed up shit in your head. Trust me with it all."

"Ian, you're making this a bigger deal than it is. I don't have any big secrets from you!" She pressed her face toward his, but he pulled back from her kiss.

"But you've got enough doubt and twisted thoughts in

there to stop you from coming straight to me when you saw the money missing?"

"I didn't know... How could I know if that was the right thing to do?"

He leaned in again, eyebrows flared, eyes dark. "Because I'm your husband?"

The words tugged low in her pelvis. Oh, how she wished that was enough. "Husbands do wrong by their wives all the time."

"I don't!" He almost shouted the word, and she flinched back. He swore under his breath. "You saw an empty bank account. You heard something out of context, and in that moment, it sounded bad. You reacted. That's understandable. But you need to listen to me before this goes someplace we can't get back from."

He was right. He'd never given her any reason to doubt him. With little to go on, she'd thought the worst. Worse than that, she'd already let herself slip into a position where that was too damn easy. "I'm sorry." It was weak, but it was something.

Not enough, though. He shook his head slowly, his expression twisting into a grim frown. "No." He pulled back a few inches and just stared at her, his gaze flickering as he thought about what to say next. She didn't expect it to be nothing, and let out a sharp gasp as he jerked himself upright, his strong upper body lifting itself into the air.

"Ian, wait—"

"Carrie." His tone pulled her up short, a warning that she couldn't quite decipher but a warning nonetheless. Now they were both pissed off, the opposite of what she wanted, and she ached at the loss of his nearness.

The sight of Carrie kneeling on the bed, her face flushed and tear-stained, her heart wounded over nothing but a stupid misunderstanding...it was more than he could handle. More than he could comprehend.

He almost hadn't come after her.

When he realized she'd called from his mother's phone, he tried to call back, but she didn't answer. The landline at his parents' farm was busy, so he'd hopped on his bike and headed back. His mom called him as he reached the outskirts of town and told him Carrie had left suddenly, and she'd keep the kids overnight if he wanted. She knew more than he did, clearly, as she asked if everything was alright and he'd dumbly told her all was fine.

It fucking was not. Damn it all to hell.

He stepped further back from the bed, needing a bit of room to think. He should just tell her. It was such a stupid misunderstanding.

He softened his voice. "Carrie, I'm the one who should be sorry. I just wanted to take care of you."

"I don't want you to take care of me!"

"Non-negotiable, babe. That's my role."

"How is keeping me in the dark about money taking care of me?"

Damn. "That's complicated."

"No, it's not."

"I wrote a cheque. I wasn't expecting it to clear that quickly."

Her eyes flashed. He thought that would have been sufficient information, that he wasn't hording the money in a secret account. He thought wrong. She clenched her fists by her side, shaking as she enunciated each word. "Who did you write a three thousand dollar cheque to, Ian?"

"I promise I'll tell you soon—"

"Tell me now." She sat back on her heels and squared her shoulders. Her voice still had a slight waver to it, but bravery had overtaken uncertainty. Fierce and brave, he could handle. Fuck, he should be able to handle it all. He should have seen this coming.

"I've let you down."

"Ian. Now. Money. Where is it?"

"No." He smiled at the flash in her eyes. "I promise, I'll show you by the end of the night. But we have some work to do on us before we worry about anything out there."

Ian couldn't remember ever rendering his wife speechless before, and he regretted that this was not a moment to savour. A speechless Carrie was pretty entertaining. Her eyes were bright teal today, made so by coloured contacts, another quirky Carrie-ism that made her stand out in any crowd, but especially in Wardham. At this particular moment, they were practically glowing in the afternoon light, a trick of unshed tears and heightened emotions on both their parts, and he wanted nothing more than to cross to her and kiss her fears away.

"Carrie, do you believe me?"

Her eyes narrowed in thought, and she cocked her head to the side. "Yes."

"So that's progress." He lifted his hand waved off her protest. "I'm sorry for asking if you trusted me when I came home. That wasn't the right moment."

"I don't like fighting with you, honey." She reached her hands out to him and wiggled her fingers.

Habit almost had him accept the gesture, but he caught himself. "Babe, we still need to talk."

"Can we hug while we do it?" Fuck, there was no way he could say no to that. He did her one better, crossing to the bed and sweeping her up in his arms, then turned and pulled her down to lie in the crook of his arm. He tangled one hand into her hair and stroked her arm lazily with the other.

After savouring the embrace for a minute, he plowed ahead. He didn't know where to start. "Tell me everything that was going on in your head today."

She snorted. "That's an awful lot."

He shrugged. He'd rehash the grocery list if it would help.

"I was thinking about the night we met." She took a deep breath. "You were something else."

Something she hadn't been looking for. He'd been making up for that for a long time. Maybe she'd never get over it. She was stuck with him, so that was her tough luck.

"You had the sexiest tan lines. They followed the curve of your muscles perfectly, and the rest of you wasn't lilywhite at all, but your arms...you clearly spent all of your time outside. So the muscles were legit, and you were so comfortable in your skin, it was infectious."

"Babe, that's not the problematic part of your thinking."

"I'm getting there." She tilted her face up to look him in the eye. "Because I'm about to say something really...harsh, and I want you to know that I was stupid. That I know better now, and I love you, with all of my heart."

A quick reassurance almost slipped out of his mouth, but they'd done too much glossing over. "Go on."

"Do you remember our second date?"

"The arts festival, by the river." She'd bought a hideous painting, and he'd made a dumb-ass comment about it being a waste of money. She almost hadn't invited him in at the end of the night.

"Let's just say, the success of that night was entirely achieved in the overnight portion. Which is the only reason there was a third date." She squirmed against his side.

"And on our third date..." A rush of memories flooded over him. "Fuck, on our third date, you told me you thought I wanted six kids and a barefoot and pregnant wife in the kitchen of a ramshackle farmhouse."

He'd asked her to come see his parents' farm, and she'd brushed him off. She hadn't invited him in that night. "I didn't think you were going to see me again."

She froze next to him. Ah. The nugget of truth at the heart of the anecdote.

"Carrie," he put as much love as he could into her name and the words that followed. "Babe, I don't care how we got here."

"You wanted to know what I was thinking about."

"I did. I do."

"I was re-hashing. How precarious our relationship was in the beginning. Thinking about how we didn't use condoms the last couple of times we had sex. And how I felt about that. Remembering..."

"How do you feel about it?"

Another deep breath, this one longer than the last. "Anxious."

"Then why didn't you say—"

"I don't know!"

"Yes, you do. Carrie, don't pretend with me. Not anymore." He rolled on top of her, wanting to be face-to-face for this conversation. Without an option to run away. He braced himself up on his forearms and stroked her hair. The tender gesture also conveniently pushed her gaze back to his.

"There's a part of me that will always want your babies, Ian." She blushed, and he had to stifle a pretty strong caveman reaction because he could guess what was coming next, and he wanted—needed—her to know he understood.

"But you're done." She sucked in a breath, and he dipped his head, nudging her nose with his. "You ninny. Why didn't you tell me?"

"Because you want six kids and a barefoot and pregnant wife in the kitchen of a ramshackle farmhouse. Because you fell in love with me when Kaylie was born, and I'm worried that as Drew gets older, you'll regret not having more kids. Resent me for it, and we'll grow apart." The floodgates were open, and he'd asked for it, so he couldn't very well tell her to stop. But he needed to address one important point before she continued.

"Babe, come here." He rolled to his side and tugged Carrie with him, pulling her into his lap as he sat up against the headboard. He splayed his hands wide around her waist and squeezed. How could she doubt his adoration? Or think for a second that he wasn't the one who would be begging her not to leave him at some point? There was more that needed to be said. More that should have been said a long time ago. "Do you know why I told you that I thought that painting was ugly?"

She laughed at the memory. "I can't possibly imagine.

That was a really dumb thing to say when I so clearly liked it."

"Babe, it was awful."

"Was not."

"Was too. And I couldn't imagine where it would go in our ramshackle farmhouse."

"Seriously, it was cu—" She cut herself off and licked her lips. "What?"

"I forgot that it was our second date. I'd wandered over to the next stall, it sold jewelry or something, and I turned back, and there you were. Glorious and bold and full of life in a way I didn't know was possible until I met you. You took my breath away, and I knew in that moment that I wanted to spend the rest of my life with you. I walked over, wrapped my arms around your waist, and you turned to me and said—"

"Isn't this fantastic?" Carrie whispered, her eyes wide and wet. "And you said, 'Babe, seriously? I wouldn't put that in my outhouse.'"

"Not my finest moment."

"You meant our outhouse." She was piecing together what he should just come out and say, but the look on her face...he wanted to remember it forever.

"Yeah." He slid his hands around to her back and traced up her spine, pressing her torso towards his a little bit more with each step of his fingertips. "Date two, angel, and I could see our future so clearly that it didn't occur to me to be nice about the painting."

"How have I never known this?" She whispered the question against his lips, and instead of answering, he pressed a hot, hungry kiss against her mouth and was rewarded with a happy little sigh.

"I was distracted, but I wasn't stupid. I knew you weren't as into me as I was…well, and then when you got pregnant, I thought I'd have a battle on my hands getting you to marry me. Even when you agreed, I knew we weren't doing it for the same reasons. And then we had more important things to worry about."

"And when you offered me a divorce?"

"I told myself I just wanted you to be happy. That was a total lie, by the way." He nipped at her bottom lip, and she parted for him. Always so willing. His heart swelled. "I wasn't done convincing you to love me. I don't know what I would have done if you'd said yes to a divorce, but it wouldn't have been pretty."

"I already loved you, you know." She eased back to look him in the eye. "I don't know when it happened, but at some point over that awful summer, you took up permanent residence in my heart."

"Why did you think I didn't love you until Kaylie was born?" Her tongue had darted out to lick her lips a few times, and he was getting distracted from his original purpose. *Focus.*

"You didn't say it until that night in the hospital." Her words smacked him in the chest like a two-by-four. That couldn't be right. His disbelief must have scrawled across his face in neon letters, because she shrugged. "It's not a big deal."

As carefully as he could, given the itchy panic crawling rapidly through his chest, he flipped her over to her back and dragged his hands to her face. "Babe, it's a big deal. I love you. I love you to the moon and back, and all that crap we tell the kids. I love you so much it hurts when I don't get home for fucking dinner. I've loved you since our second date, and I've wasted eight years of not telling you. That's part of what's been creeping through your head, isn't it?"

She shook her head against his hands. "No."

"Truth, babe."

"I know you love me."

"But?"

She shrugged. "But nothing. You show me that you love me, and that's enough."

He lowered himself over her like a blanket and buried his face in her neck. "You deserve more than that."

Her lips moved against his temple, her breath warm and soft. "I have more than I ever dreamed possible."

"You don't have Europe."

"We'll get there some day. Maybe when we retire." She laughed. "Who am I kidding? You'll never retire. Maybe Drew will take over the farm one day. Or maybe Kaylie will like to travel, and we can leave you boys behind. Or I could go on my own once Drew is in school—ooof!" Carrie rubbed her stomach where he'd shouldered her in his haste to jump off the bed.

"Sorry, babe. Get up, we're going for a ride."

"Ian, what's going on?"

He grabbed her hand and pulled her toward the door, scooping up his boots on the way. "It's time for me to show you what I should have just told you about in the first place."

5

———

It wasn't easy dragging her away from a big bed in an empty house, but there would be time for hot make-up sex later. Right now, they had one final secret to deal with.

When was the last time she'd been on the back of his bike? Too long. On the weekend, he'd make time for them to go on a ride together. See the fall colours. Whatever. Just have her legs wrapped around his hips, her breasts pressed into his back, for more than the two minute hop into town. This was going to be a tease, but a worthwhile one.

He pulled out his phone to text Evan then thought better of it. Both West brothers would be at work. Which was a sweet ride to the far side of town and back. Even better.

When she stepped out of the house, decked out in snug faded jeans tucked into knee-high leather boots and a curve-hugging white nylon jacket that managed to zip up to her neck and still show off her gorgeous rack, he was tempted to abandon the plan and slide right back inside for the rest of the afternoon. Inside the house. Inside Carrie.

Instead, he satisfied his base urges with a low wolf-whistle, and he didn't bother telling his chubby to go away. She shot him a shy smile that turned not so shy as she gave him her own once over and lingered on his growing erection.

"Looking forward to taking me for a ride?" Her wide eyes looked innocent, but he knew better.

"Don't tease me, Carrie, or I'll have you back inside and naked in less than a minute." His strut was partially put on, but the rush and confusion of the day's events had him on edge. He had something to prove, to himself and Carrie, and he was going to do it in a way that left no doubt. About his feelings, or his role in her life.

"I'm not teasing. Much. It's just you look..." She trailed off with a grin. He felt it too, a hum of energy between them. "You look good. All long legs and tough-guy leather."

He widened his stance as she took two sauntering steps into his personal space. Not that he wouldn't gladly share it with her. *What's mine is hers, in every way.* Which reminded him that they needed to go but not before he savoured the feel of her body pressed against his, her warm, wet mouth softening against his. The taste of excitement on her lips. He tugged her hair gently then gave her one final kiss before sliding his leg over the bike and gesturing for her to join him.

Go West Winery was past the bluffs on the east end of town. It had originally been built as an estate, and the vines a hobby, but Ty and Evan West had picked it up for a song after it had been abandoned. They'd just finished building a new main hall, with a tasting room, space for formal events, offices, and a large scale production wing. The original estate buildings were at the far end of the property, currently being used as a bachelor pad by the brothers, but Kyle had told him that the next phase of expansion was to hire someone to run the mansion as an inn.

There weren't a lot of cars in the lot, but he recognized Evan's SUV, and put down his kick stand. He could feel Carrie's confusion radiating against his back, but he wasn't going to give her a chance to pin him down. She eased off the bike first, then he joined her, but before she could say anything, he traced his index finger up her zipper and tapped on her chin before resting it against her lips. "Contain yourself, babe. Wait here, I'll be right back."

———

She truly had no idea what was going on, and it was exhilarating. Just an hour ago, she'd been scared. Now...why had they not talked earlier? How had they not talked about some of that earlier? Life was busy, sure, but too busy to spend any time recollecting about their early days?

Maybe if their early days together had followed a more typical path. Maybe if they'd each been more confident that their relationship wasn't just perched on a precarious foundation of happenstance. When really, their love had cemented what started so shakily. Maybe that was the issue—they had never talked about it out of love.

How messed up. She shook her head. And now he was being cagey and secretive, but with the bright promise of disclosure looming, she could be patient. Try to be patient. Sheesh. How long was he going to be inside?

She made it halfway to the large glass doors when he strode out. Good lord, he was a sight. Dusty black boots. Snug jeans, loose t-shirt, except for where it stretched over his round shoulders. Long arms, corded with muscle. One of them, pointing straight at her. Oh shit.

"I wasn't coming inside." Her protest was totally weak.

"Babe." He snorted and tucked her under his arm, turning them back toward the bike.

"I can't help but be curious. Why are we here, if we're not staying?"

"Had to pick something up."

He didn't have anything in his arms, just her on one side, and his jacket tossed over his other shoulder. That meant...

"Get out of my pockets." A laugh rumbled through his chest as she searched him. His keys were in one front pocket, his wallet in the back. Nothing else. "Seriously, angel, time to go. Unless you want me to search you?" He pulled her tight against his front and tugged at her zipper. "I've been wanting to see what you've got on under this jacket since you stepped out of the house."

"It's not nothing this time," she teased. "But it's something."

"Something that will have to wait. Hop on."

Riding on the back of Ian's bike was, in a word, awesome. He didn't have a motorcycle when they met. He'd seemed as white-bread wholesome as Canadian farm boys come when they met, even though at twenty-six, he'd hardly been a boy. But he'd had a secret account he'd been saving for quite a while, a fact she discovered one night when she was in the midst of her second-trimester horniness and Ian had convinced her it was a good idea to share sexual fantasies. He wasn't wrong. When she told him she had a mystery biker fantasy, he got a wicked gleam in his eye and told her in minute detail just what kind of bike he'd ride. He even detailed a totally impractical and very hot biker babe outfit that she'd be wearing when he'd sweep her off her feet, and they both enjoyed her response. But when Kaylie was born, he'd put the money he'd been saving into an education fund. Next came a mortgage, but when she was pregnant with Drew, and it was time to replace his truck, she managed to convince him that she was really okay with him getting a bike instead. It appealed to his practical side, being cheaper to buy, and more affordable on gas. But they both knew that it also appealed to his secret inner bad boy. It was months before she got to ride on the back of it, and when she did, it was every bit as awesome as their shared fantasy predicted, even with the more sensible outfit.

A few years hadn't changed that. The wind rushing against the few bits of exposed skin. Cold air all around her, except where Ian's hard back warmed up her front. The roar of the machine between her legs. It was hot as hell.

The winery was on the north side of the east/west running road that, after a kilometre, turned into Heritage Street, one of two main streets in downtown Wardham. The other, creatively named Main Street, was the north/south street that intersected Heritage before ending at the municipal beach. A block before they reached Main, Ian turned the bike north, away from the beach and toward the park surrounding the town hall. If Wardham had a central business district, this was the heart of it. A quick left turn down a private lane, and they found themselves in the small parking lot in the center of the block behind Wardham Grocery and the now empty and derelict storefronts immediately beside it.

Ian pulled her toward the back entrance of the empty

store two doors down from the grocery store, kicking up dust as he hurried along.

"Honey, what are we—" Carrie didn't get a chance to finish her question before Ian pulled out his keys, flipped through the bundle, and after he found the shiny silver one he wanted, he held it out to her.

"Try it." He set his big hand in the small of her back and gave her a gentle shove toward the door.

The key slid smoothly into the lock. The door and the handle both looked new—just about the only part of the building that did. Inside, a long expanse of dark greeted them. They were in a narrow hallway with doors at the end. As her eyes adjusted to the dark, she realized that the space immediately next to the door was wider than the hall in front of them, more like a store room.

"This used to be the five and dime, right?" She didn't know why she was whispering. It was the middle of the afternoon, and Ian had a key. But there was something wondrous about this moment that she didn't want to risk with a raised voice.

Ian pressed in tight against her back, his hands resting loosely at her waist. His voice was warm and low in her ear. "Yep. Then it was used seasonally by H&R Block for tax prep season. Remember that year that I worked for them in the spring?"

Kaylie had been a baby, and they'd moved in with his parents. It hadn't been a great winter. Ian had taken the extra job to speed up the down payment savings. "Right. Doesn't this place have a great exposed brick wall?"

He nodded against the top of her head. "Come on, let's go out front."

The doors on either side of the hall looked like bathrooms, but the middle door opened into a small anteroom with an open window to the front of the store. They walked through that, Ian pausing to find the light switch, but they didn't need it, as the afternoon sun was spilling in the large front windows, two of them, bracketing a big door. She twirled in the wide space, taking in the creaky old wood floors and exposed brick on the wall around the door they'd just stepped through.

"Ian, it's fantastic!" She slowed her spin and clapped her hands. "Ty and Evan own this?"

He nodded. "Just Evan, actually. He bought this building and the one next door. But he doesn't have a plan for them yet. No time to find tenants or renovate."

She sighed. "It's a lot of work. I hope he finds someone who's willing to do something different, though. Something that will draw people into town."

"Like what?" He was watching her with a small smile. It had been too long since they'd talked about the potential of the town. She loved the unlimited potential of fantasy, and he seemed to have infinite patience for listening to her prattle on.

"I don't know... A flower shop, maybe. Oooh, an ice cream and candy store! If it were mine, I'd do a bakery." She paced toward the back of the shop. "A glass display here. And a higher bar, over here, with a couple of stools, for people waiting for coffee. Yes, espresso and hot chocolate, maybe Italian sodas too. Keep it simple. No tables, you want people to take their drinks and wander down the strip."

"There's a strip?" His grin was bigger now, his teeth white against the late fall tan farmers get.

"There would be. Wardham has the potential to be a big draw. Beautiful small town, gorgeous beach, close to the city. But we need to have services that make their visit special. Memorable."

"Like a bakery-slash-coffee shop."

"Exactly."

"What would you call it?"

She laughed. "A Bun In The Oven."

"And this space would be perfect for it?"

She shrugged. "Sure. It would take a lot of renovating, turn that middle room into a kitchen, or maybe the back, and storage in the middle...but first Evan would need to find someone crazy enough to see the potential."

"I don't think you're crazy, babe."

"Well, no, but for me it's just a fantas—" She broke off, the end of the word jammed in her throat. Three thousand dollars. A key. "Ian?" His name squeaked past the lump.

"Yeah, babe?"

She gulped a breath. "What did you do?"

He grinned again, biggest smile ever this time. "I've leased this space from Evan. I'm going to renovate it, over the winter, and in the spring, either you're going to open A Bun In The Oven, or we'll sublet it to someone else to recoup our investment."

She couldn't breathe. "This was your secret."

"I should have told you."

"This was your secret?" She shrieked the words again, and she felt bad about that, because shrieks could be taken a couple of different ways, she wanted it to be clear that she liked this plan. She liked this plan a lot. She hopped up and down and clapped her hands together. "Oh my god."

"You like it." Relief flooded his voice.

"Honey, I love it. We're definitely crazy, together, it's not just me now, you're whole hog crazy too, but yes, I like it." She grabbed his hands. "You're okay with me doing this? No more babies, just a business baby?"

He nodded and curved his hands around her waist. "Time for me to share you with the world, babe."

"I can't believe it." She danced on the spot again, tapping her hands against his chest. "You knew I wanted this?"

"Of course."

"What do you mean, of course? Here I was having a panic attack because I didn't know if you loved me for being anything more than the mother of your children, and you were doing this?" She glowered at him, but it had no heat. Unlike the look he shot right back, which was full of heat. The good kind.

"That you are the mother of my children will always be a part of why I love you." He nudged a growing erection into her belly. "But it wasn't the first reason I loved you, and it won't be the last. And it's definitely not the most important, which is that you are simply amazing. Carrie Nixon, you are loved for being you." He shifted his hands lower, cupping her ass, and she arched her back. "You are wanted. And needed. For being you."

She moaned as he nudged into the vee of her legs. "I never imagined...part of my heart has been stuck in that moment, eight years ago, when I told you that I was pregnant and I didn't know what you were going to do."

"Between then and now, a lifetime has happened. Neither of us are those scared kids anymore. And thank fuck for that."

With a quick bend of the knee, he had her up in the air before she could holler.

"Oh my god, Ian, put me down." Her thighs shook as she tightened them around his waist, but he stood there in the middle of the dusty, empty storefront, like a billygoat on the mountainside. Surefooted and utterly confident. "I am not... this is not a good idea."

"Carrie. I've got you." He grinned at her. "Give me a kiss."

She licked her lips and traced her hands around his face. Along his scruffy jawline, and down his neck.

"Babe, kiss me. Or I'm going to kiss you, and I'm not going to stop until we've christened this place."

"That sounds like a great idea." The words were breathy and hopeful, and totally lost as their mouths collided.

EPILOGUE

They didn't actually christen Bun that afternoon, because it was afternoon, and the light in the back room was burnt out, and they were grownups with an empty house and a big bed available just a few minutes away. They made out for a while, though, delicious hot kisses interspersed with new ideas for the store and distracted gropings.

The next few months had been a whirlwind of activity, but they'd pulled it off. Permits filed, inspections completed. Opening day wasn't going to be a full range of products, just muffins, baked last night, and scones, which needed to go into the oven in three hours.

She should go back to sleep for a bit, but it was raining. Opening day, and there was a steady downpour outside. No way could she go back to sleep. Next to her, Ian shifted, his warm hand snaking out from under the quilt to cup her breast. She smiled and sank in her back into him.

"Can't sleep?" He murmured the question into the soft

spot between her shoulder and her neck, and the nerves in her stomach were smothered by a different kind of tension.

"Mmmm."

His tongued darted out to taste her skin, a wet swipe followed by cold air hitting her skin, and then his mouth again, licking and nibbling. Her eyes rolled up at the sensation, and she let out a small sigh. His thumb rolled over her nipple, and she lifted her top leg, hooking it over his behind her. "Eager, babe?"

"Always."

"What do you want?" His mouth had shifted to the back of her neck now, and he bit her lightly when she didn't immediately respond. She couldn't. Nibbling her neck and playing with her nipple may just be foreplay, but it was really awesome foreplay.

"Uhm..." She groaned as he pinched her nipple. "Stop it."

"If you wanted me to stop, you wouldn't thrust your ass against my cock like that when I do it." He tapped her nipple with the pad of one of his fingers, and dragged his hand down her quivering belly, murmuring appreciative words into her hair on his way to her core. "You're so soft, angel, so sweet and soft and wet."

"You do that to me, Ian. It's all you."

"No, babe. It's all you. What do you want?"

She squirmed under his dancing fingers. "Your mouth."

Behind her, his cock flexed in approval of this plan. "Fuck, yeah." He rolled onto his back, pulling away from her, but used his closer arm to flip her over. "Climb up here."

When he'd moved into her tiny apartment over the laundromat, he'd told her that one day they'd have a big bed with a big headboard. Having never had a real bed, just a mattress on a frame, Carrie had smiled and nodded. No way would they waste money on a headboard, not with an unexpected young family to figure out how to support.

The first time he'd suggested she ride his face, she'd wished for a headboard. The next time, it was to celebrate the purchase of their first real bed. Now she braced herself against the much beloved piece of furniture, and gasped as his tongue made first contact with her sex. He growled in delight, and she reached down to part her folds, but he nudged her hand out of the way. "Your big day, babe, let me do all the work."

It didn't take long. He teased her at first, licking around in lazy loops, avoiding her clit until she couldn't help but squirm, and then he swirled his tongue around that swollen nub, flicking and sucking it until she thought she would explode, and then he started moving his hands up and around her hips, down her ass and even trailing through that cleft, totally disorienting her, so when her orgasm hit, it was almost a surprise, an upending wave. She shuddered hard against the wood frame in front of her, and Ian lifted her leg enough to roll out from underneath her. He tugged the quilt loose from the rest of the bedding and pulled it up and around their sweat-slicked bodies.

She shook again against his side, and practically purred when he rubbed her back. The rain was coming down harder now, that unwavering percussion the only sound in the otherwise quiet night. The aftershocks of her climax continued to ripple through her body, and she was still achingly aware of her desire for her husband. Under the warm blanket, she reached for his erection, which leapt back to full-strength at her gentle stroke.

"Do you have time?" His hand tightened on her side.

She'd make time. "Come join me in the shower?"

The quilt hit the floor, and Ian dashed to the bathroom. By the time she sauntered in, the shower was steamy.

"You know, I'm not in that much of a rush."

He grinned. "Yeah, but I am." They soaped each other up then rinsed off with a slow fuck against the tile wall, under the full force of the shower spray. They shared a look full of history and hope as he came inside her, his hips holding her up. At one time, they'd reveled in that act because it gave them babies and built their family. Now that they'd made a permanent decision about birth control, it was just for them, their secret intimacy that had no other purpose than to be as one in that moment.

———

When Ian woke up the second time, it wasn't to the warm rub of his wife's nipple in his palm. Too bad, that. But it was possibly the second best way to be woken up. Two kids piled hard on him, one tackling his head, the other aiming straight for his kidneys.

"Daddy! It's time to go to Mommy's store! It's muffin time!" Kaylie had probably been up almost as long as Carrie, but she'd been warned on pain of losing all muffins, ever, not to wake up her younger brother. Drew was not a morning kid.

But now he, too, was bouncing merrily around on the bed. "Mwuffins! Mwuffins!"

Ian didn't need to be told again. He was pretty excited as well. He oversaw face scrubbing and teeth brushing, made sure that Drew's underwear was on the right way, and Kaylie had enough change in her purse to buy them all muffins and steamed milk. Ian's would have a few shots of espresso added, since his sexpot wife had interrupted his beauty sleep.

They loaded into his brand new truck—with Carrie doing early mornings at the shop, he was on kid duty again, and she didn't want to drive the bike to work in the winter—and set off for town.

"Dad." Kaylie only called him that when she wanted to be taken seriously. "I think there's a problem."

"What's that, sweetie?" They drove past the shop and doubled back, looking for a parking spot.

"Mom's shop isn't big enough." Her little finger tapped firmly on the window facing the bakery. A large hanging sign had just been installed the day before, a giant red coffee mug with the word BUN underneath it. The full name of the store was painted on one of the front windows. "Bakery & Coffee Shop" was spelled out on the other. But you couldn't see that right now, because there was a large crowd on the sidewalk.

The rain had stopped sometime earlier, although many people in the crowd had umbrellas, just in case. His heart swelled. They were there for Carrie, no matter what.

He leaned over and ruffled Kaylie's hair. She glowered at him and he laughed. "Mommy's shop is the perfect size. She won't have this many people every day."

"Not with an attitude like that, she won't!" Kaylie crossed her arms over her chest and looked fierce.

"You know what, kiddo? You're absolutely right."

THE END

Thank you for visiting Wardham! If you liked this book, please leave a review (either for this story or the entire set) and help other readers discover a new author.

Want more? Up next is Laney and Kyle's story...a love affair paused for a decade that explodes at Christmas. Turn the page!

I also have a mailing list that I use to give readers a heads-up about new releases and big sales. If you sign up, you'll also be given an opportunity to read new releases before they hit stores!

—Zoe

WHAT ONCE WAS PERFECT

AN EXCERPT

Chapter One

Kyle Nixon grabbed the empty bowl of chips from his coffee table and kicked his brother's feet out of the way as he headed for the kitchen.

"That's no way to treat your guests, especially when they're the ones who provided the entertainment in the first place," Ian groused, but his grin belied any grumpiness. Kyle knew his older brother was just happy to have a rare afternoon for vegging out on the couch and playing the latest first-person shooter game. Ever since his daughter fell behind in her reading homework, Ian's wife Carrie had banned video games from their farmhouse.

As a teacher, Kyle understood.

As a gamer, though, he felt his brother's pain.

The obvious solution had been for Kyle to selflessly volunteer to house the brand new PlayStation at his own place. He was generous like that. It looked fan-fucking-tastic next to his Xbox.

A knock at the door interrupted his search through his pantry for more snacks. "Evan's here."

"He'll let himself in," Ian mumbled between shots fired.

He would. Kyle's half-renovated schoolhouse just outside of their small lakeside town had become the de facto bachelor hang-out pad, even though Evan had just built a killer house on the bluffs overlooking his winery.

The Nixon and West brothers were now from two different worlds, but they were still the best of friends. Video games and beer had a way of bonding guys for life like that.

Before Kyle could holler that the door was open, Evan was inside, kicking the first snow of the year off his boots. "I'm moving to Hawaii."

"You'd miss us too much."

"They have people in bikinis and board shorts there, year round. You assholes don't compete with that kind of eye candy."

Kyle snorted. "Then go."

Evan growled something about too much work to do and threw himself onto the couch next to Ian. Two grumpy old men. They deserved each other as best friends.

He resumed his search for snacks. "I've got pretzels. Maybe we should order in some pizzas."

"Already on it," Evan said over his shoulder, his eyes not leaving the TV screen. "Ty's in the city. He's picking up dinner on his way here."

Kyle grabbed his phone and shot off a quick text that they needed more beer. It was shaping up to be that kind of afternoon.

The fucking awesome kind.

If his brother and best friends weren't there, he'd...what? Probably finish the trim along the far wall. Maybe get started on the framing off of his bedroom, which was currently just blocked off by a heavy curtain.

He liked carpentry, but it was a poor substitute for human company.

Time to start dating again. But the way things had ended with Crystal, he wanted to have his head on straight.

As long as his fingers twitched to type Laney Calhoun's name into the search bar on his Internet browser, he wasn't ready.

It had taken a Herculean effort not to stalk her online. He knew she was in Chicago now. Five hour drive if traffic was kind. Just across the Canada-US border.

Laney Calhoun. Whip-smart, beautiful beyond measure. Hated his guts. Still owned a tiny bit of real estate on his heart and probably always would, because he was a fool.

He'd hurt her so badly she hadn't come back to Wardham for longer than a weekend visit in more than a decade.

And the only time they'd seen each other, in a crowded room at her father's funeral, he'd found himself at a loss for words.

He took a deep breath and shook it off. It was for the best that Crystal had left him. And it was for the best that he get over Laney and move on with his life.

He'd done it once. And now he was doing it again. He squeezed his hands on the edge of the granite countertop. He'd renovated this house up from an empty shell. Designed the kitchen himself. Installed a wood stove in the living room and hung a big screen TV, flanked on either side by bookshelves. It was warm and cozy and the best damn bachelor pad a geek could ever want.

Now he just needed to get his head back in the game and find a woman to drag back to his lair.

———

"Mr. Nixon!"

Kyle suppressed a grin as the eager ten-year-old hopped up and down in front of him. "Yes, Michaela?"

"Andrew's going to be late, but he has a good reason."

"Yeah?" He hovered his pen over the attendance sheet. "Did you see him this morning?"

She nodded, dancing back and forth on her feet. It was four days before the Christmas break. They were all a little antsy. "His mom is taking him to the grocery store to get some canned goods for the food drive."

And the hidden grin fell away. *Shit.* Andrew's mother worked two jobs and the last thing she needed to do was buy food to keep up with the Joneses. He hated the messages that the school sent home. Yes, it was important to collect donations for the food bank. But promising the kids that the class with the biggest donation pile would get a pizza lunch on the last day of school before the break...

He gritted his teeth and gave Michaela a smile. "Thanks. I'll hold off on ten minutes before sending this down." Andrew didn't need another late recorded on his file, either. He cleared his throat and lifted his voice. "Does everyone have their planner out? Good. As soon as the announcements and anthem are over, please write down these three notes for your parents to read." He pointed at the smart board. "And once you've got that done, find your free reading book for the week. I want everyone to have at least one chapter read before we move on to the science lesson."

As the intercom squawked to life, the door flung open and Andrew hurried through. Kyle gave him a welcoming wave and marked him as present. "And who wants to take the attendance down to the office?"

———

At the end of the day, he straightened up his classroom and finished his notes on the reading assessments he'd done on two students that day. One was just fine, but the other was falling behind. He'd bring it up with the reading resource teacher the next day, but tonight he had something just as important to do.

He drove the few blocks from the school to Wardham's main drag and parked in front of his sister-in-law's bakery. He'd grab some coffee and muffins once he'd done this one little good deed.

At least he hoped it was a good idea.

Karen Miller wouldn't hesitate to tell him if he was on the wrong track. And she'd keep his secret if it was a good plan.

He found her in the back office at Wardham Grocery, and knocked on the open door. She glanced up from her computer. "Hey."

Karen had been a year between Ian and Kyle at school, and he'd always liked her. *Date this one*, his brain said. She was pretty and smart and kind, and just as much a homebody as Kyle was. Karen would never leave Wardham. She wasn't destined for Harvard and a big-city career as a surgeon.

But his heart didn't leap at the warm, welcoming smile on the other side of the desk. And in the thirty years they'd known each other, not once had she ever shown any interest in him beyond board game nights and trading library book recommendations back and forth.

"Earth to Kyle..."

He laughed and shook his head. "Sorry. Long day."

She tilted her head to the side. "What's up?"

"I need a favour, and I'm treading close to the line in even talking about this with you, so I don't want you to ask me why and this has to stay between us."

Her eyebrows hit the roof. "Okay."

"For real."

"I only gossip about your dating life. Mum's the word if it's anything else."

"No worries on that front." He took a deep breath. "You pay pretty close attention to who's in the shop, right? Work the front cash sometimes, that kind of thing?"

She nodded. "Of course. For the gossip." She winked. "And other reasons."

"One of my students...I'd like his mother to win a gift card that I'll pay for. Tell her it's the person who shopped just before her, or she's the random hundredth shopper of the day, something like that."

"We rarely get a hundred shoppers in a single day."

"Week, then. You know what I mean."

Her eyes went soft and she dropped the teasing tone. "I do. Who's the student?"

He hesitated, then gave her Andrew's mother's full name.

Instantly, she was out of her chair and her arms were

wrapped around his neck. "Kyle Nixon, you're a good fucking egg, you know that?"

He laughed and returned her hug. "Tell my mom that."

"I will. And then we'll find you a nice girl to settle down with."

"Nope, don't do that."

"Too late, already on it." She squeezed him tight, then stepped back. "Just tell me how much and consider it done. She's in here a few times a week."

"Thanks. I owe you one."

"Not at all. Happy to help. Tis the season, and all that."

Chapter Two

Laney slid her laptop into her leather messenger bag and flicked off the overhead light in her office. She paused at her secretary's desk to steal a peppermint chocolate square and drop off a light blue jewelry box wrapped in a white ribbon. One of the perks of living and working in downtown Chicago—easy access to awesome shopping.

The tap and scratch of pen on paper sounded from across the hall and she hesitated. She could sneak out, but she wanted this resolved before the holidays. The affair with Rick had been a mistake from the beginning, they were on the same page about that, but how do you move back to just being friends and colleagues?

The door pushed open as she knocked, and Rick looked up from his desk. "You're off, then?"

"Yep. I just wanted to say...Merry Christmas."

"You sure I can't convince you to come to the lake house with me?"

She shook her head with a rueful smile. "Let's not do this again, Rick. I'm not the girl you should take home to meet your mom."

"I know. Woulda been convenient if you were." He returned her bittersweet expression and gestured for her to take a seat. "Don't you ever want more, though?"

"I...I used to." She sagged into one of the two chairs across from him and scrubbed her face with her hands. Once upon a time, she'd wanted it all. "If I was capable of falling in love, you'd be the perfect guy."

"Shame that's not how it actually works."

She bit her lip and nodded, although it wasn't like she was an expert on healthy relationships. Quite the opposite. Laney had banned emotional entanglements from her life a long time ago. Never again would she be vulnerable and give her heart to someone. It wasn't worth the pain.

She barely did physical relationships, only agreeing to enter into a sexual arrangement if the interested party understood he would need to get tested and be monogamous for the duration. Condoms and birth control were mandatory. Most men cooled off in a hurry when they heard those terms. Rick had chuckled and scheduled a follow up discussion for a week later, when he presented her with a clean bill of health.

They joined DermaNorth at the same time a year earlier, both fresh out of plastic surgery residency programs, and she had seen him date two other women in the intervening months. Both relationships had been casual, brief and ended amicably, exactly what she liked. So they negotiated terms: Laney wanted an escort to fundraising events and didn't like overnight guests; Rick didn't want to leave in the middle of the night, but promised not to linger in the morning or expect breakfast.

"I'm sorry that I changed the rules on you."

Seriously, what kind of guy apologizes after a woman breaks up with him? Laney hated herself a little bit for not being open to exploring something more with Rick. But while their time together had been nice, that's all it had been. Physical compatibility and pleasant conversation. "What happened? Is it the holidays? More pressure from your parents?"

"Honestly? I think it was my birthday. Another year older, and what do I have to show for it?"

Laney cocked her eyebrow in disbelief. "Your career?"

"There's gotta be more to life than this, Laney." His lips quirked, then he cleared his throat. "Well, for us mere mortals, anyway."

"Hey! I have a life outside work." She paused, then dipped her head, acknowledging the point. "Okay, I don't, but—"

He interrupted her with a chuckle and she feigned a glower before continuing. "I get it, I really do. You want someone to come home to at the end of the day, even if it's in the middle of the night and all they do is rub your back for a minute after you stumble to bed. Someone who knows that when you scratch your nose at family dinners, it means you need to be rescued. Someone who can read your moods and bring you wine or chocolate or run you a bath without being asked. You're ready for sweatpants and watching TV on the couch, and loving every minute of it."

He stared at her, and she realized her voice had drifted to a whisper. "Holy shit."

"What?"

"Laney Calhoun, you've been in love before."

"Shut up."

"Tell me about him." He leaned forward, propped his elbows on the desk, and steepled his fingers. The wicked gleam in his eyes was annoying, but at least she didn't need to worry about leaving a broken heart behind over the holidays.

"Never going to happen." She pushed herself to a stand. "It's late, I have to go."

"Hey." Rick raised his hands, as if stop her, then dropped them to his desk. "Have a safe trip."

She inched her car forward. She'd made it to Detroit without hitting much traffic, but there was always a bit of a line at the border. Bright lights flooded the concrete area around the toll booths, obscuring the rise of the Ambassador Bridge against the early dawn sky. She counted the coins she needed again, knowing she had the right amount but indulging her obsessive nature because no one was there to make fun of her. As the truck in front eased past the toll booth onto the bridge, she rolled down her window. This routine was familiar, if not comfortable. Heading home always stirred up conflicting emotions. On the other side of the bridge lay the university. She could already feel the pang of regret that would lance through her gut as she drove past, an unavoidable reaction to a place so tied up in her memories of Kyle. The library. Their favourite Italian restaurant just off-campus. A few blocks further, and she'd pass his first apartment. It would have been her first home away from the farm if things had worked out differently.

She'd only seen him once in the last decade, at her father's funeral two years earlier. A decade had hardened her heart enough that she was able to shake his hand and ignore the liquid warmth that slithered up her arm. Able to hear his words of condolences and pretend they wouldn't ring in her ears for hours after. He stood in front of her in the church basement for a few extra moments, the line of community members paused behind him, and for a moment she thought he would say something else, but then he shook his head and moved on to give her mother a quick hug and repeat the same generic platitudes. By the time the receiving line had dwindled, he was gone. It was for the best, she had reminded herself at the time. No point in picking at old wounds. She'd learned her lesson twelve years ago, the last summer she spent in Wardham, the first summer she'd allowed herself to have a fling. The only summer she'd spent in love.

The delay wasn't significant on the other side of the bridge. Within minutes, she had pulled up to the Canadian border crossing and was handing over her identification to the guard in the booth.

"Where are you from?"

"I'm a Canadian citizen living and working in Chicago."

"Do you have any alcohol or tobacco in the car?"

"One bottle of champagne."

"Anything else to declare?"

"No."

"Welcome home." The border guard passed back her passport and waved her on.

For better or worse, Laney thought.

Traffic thinned and the first rays of a winter sun appeared on the horizon. In her rearview mirror, Windsor and the

United States behind it were still dark with night. On either side of the highway, drifts of snow spotted the fields. Lights flicked on in barns and farmhouses, and Laney kept her eyes peeled for suicidal deer as she passed the occasional stand of trees. Fifteen minutes down the highway, she took the bypass to the exit for Wardham, and despite her previous reservations, she smiled. Essex County would forever be home in her heart.

Three side roads zipped past before the home stretch. She knew this road well. The next farm belonged to the Frids, the one after that to the De Limas. The old school house on the corner had been an artist's retreat the last time she was home, but the sign was gone now. If she kept driving straight, she'd soon be in town, all six streets of it, then catch a first glimpse of Lake Erie. She used to love the town beach, calm water stretching out as far as the eye could see. As she did every time she visited, however, she turned left on Concession Road 2. She only came home to visit her family, and probably would stay at the farm until she left again for Chicago.

There, on top of a slight rise, was Evening Lane Farm. Her parents had liked to tell people that they'd named it after their daughters, but Laney and Evie knew it was the other way around. They didn't mind. The farm was beautiful, the long lane lined with oak trees leading to a gabled yellow brick house, the pastures to the east and west neatly squared off with white fence. A wide lawn stretched between the house and the two barns farther back, and the gravel drive continued past it, disappearing behind the larger barn, all the way to the bush. Her dad had loved taking them out on the wagon to choose a Christmas tree. Last year they'd picked one up at the grocery store in town. Last year, she'd only come home for two days.

The kitchen light was on already when she pulled her car to a stop beside the house. She grabbed her empty Starbucks travel mug and stepped into the frosty air.

"Delaney Calhoun, you must have driven all night!"

"Hey, Mom." She jogged to the open door and swept her mother into a big bear hug. "Look at you, you're practically disappearing on me."

Claire Calhoun blushed and patted her trim hips. "Evie has me doing Pilates five mornings a week. You're lucky today is a rest day."

"You look great." Laney hung her coat on her hook behind the kitchen door, labeled with crayon lettering her eight-year-old self had pressed into the wood, claiming that spot forever. "Coffee on?"

"Of course. Your sister and the boys will be down any minute. I thought I'd make eggs and bacon for breakfast, but Evie has a new protein pancake recipe she wants to try out instead."

Laney made a face. At least the coffee would be good.

"How's she doing, anyway?"

"Better than I am."

"I'd hope so. Her husband was a douchebag, Mom, and he didn't die. Big difference."

"I know, but there's still grief in divorce."

"They tell you that in group therapy?"

"How'd you know?" Claire smiled brightly. "I think they were also supposed to tell you that at medical school, smarty-pants."

Laney opened her mouth to point out that med school

was actually quite a long time ago, and counselling wasn't a significant part of the curriculum anyway, but she was interrupted by what sounded like a stampede of elephants coming down the stairs.

"SLOW DOWN. Seriously, Connor, you're going to kill your brother. Max, don't push him."

As if they hadn't heard their mother, two very excited little boys slid into the kitchen on sock feet and bounced into the new arrival.

"Aunt Laney, Aunt Laney, you're here!"

"Did you bring us presents?"

"We're going to get a tree today!"

"Do you want to see a magic trick?"

"You can sleep in our room if you want."

"We've been really good, don't listen to mom."

Laney collapsed into a pile of excited chatter with two of her most favourite people and beamed up at her older sister. "Hey! So we're getting a tree today?"

Connor poked her in the shoulder. "Don't forget about the presents."

Evie hauled him off the floor with a gentle reminder that eight-year-old boys should mind their manners and set good examples for their little brothers by offering to help make breakfast before they start asking about presents.

"Would you like some cardboard pancakes, Aunt Laney?"

"Why yes, Connor, I would, thank you. I love cardboard." She winked at Evie. "No cheat days over the holidays, sis?"

"Maybe for Christmas morning. But you're here for ten days. If we ate crap that long, we wouldn't have any energy to tromp through the bush, or have snowball fights, would we guys?"

Max pulled on Laney's hand. She bent down and he whispered in her ear, "I don't mind the pancakes. Grandma lets us have as much maple syrup as we want."

"Good to know," she whispered back.

 Max was right. With enough syrup, the pancakes made from egg whites, oats and cottage cheese didn't taste bad at all.

After breakfast, Laney cleared the table and ran the dishwasher. As she wiped down the counter, Evie came into the kitchen dressed in yoga pants and a long sleeve t-shirt with a puffy down vest over top. Her long blond hair was pulled into a high ponytail. They shared the same blue eyes and fair colouring, but Laney didn't see the faint lines on her older sister that she could feel on her own face. It might be time for Botox. "Where are you off to?"

"I have to run into town for a bit, I've got a group Pilates session at the studio and we're low on groceries. I'll show you the app I use on my phone, you can add stuff to the list before I get to the store."

"Multi-tasking mom, eh?"

Evie paused and grinned. "And loving every second of it. Little did I know that divorce would be the best thing that ever happened to me."

"I want to hear all about that later. What should I do while you're gone?"

"Convince the boys to get dressed? We'll go to the bush to get a tree when I get back."

Laney reached her hand out to rest on Evie's arm. "Is Mom going to be okay with that?"

"Of course! Her idea, actually. She's gone over to Ted's farm to pick up the wagon."

Chapter Three

Laney was hiding under a blanket on the couch. It had taken her an hour to corral Connor and Max into their room, and after promising them chocolate from her secret stash, they had agreed to get dressed for the day. She hadn't meant to lie down, but after her long drive a little catnap sounded perfect. She could hear faint peals of laughter, then thumping, a door opening and next, more clearly this time, Max counting. Another game of hide-and-seek. Pounding steps told her Connor planned on hiding in the attic, and she closed her eyes.

Her moment of peace was soon interrupted, not by target-seeking little boys, but a knock at the back door. Pulling the afghan around her shoulders, she padded into the kitchen. Bright light poured in the windows from the mid-morning sun. A large male body that she would recognize anywhere filled the glass window in the door. Seeing him here, on her mother's doorstep, was both familiar and completely unexpected. Her steps faltered and she stopped a few feet shy of the door.

At the funeral, he had worn a suit, and looked handsome, clean-cut and grown-up, a very different man than the college student she had loved. On her mother's doorstep in a fitted ski jacket and a wool toque, he looked like...himself. Shoulders a bit broader, maybe, but his body still looked lean and hard, even disguised by winter layers. Sunlight caught half of his stubble-flecked jaw. She could feel the rasp of his cheek against hers.

She dragged in a ragged breath and pressed her palms to her side. Her pulse felt thready, and she wondered if she might pass out. Fight or flight? No, Laney would faint. She closed her eyes and willed herself to not see him as a threat. Their last encounter had been entirely reasonable. She'd been distracted by grief and they'd been surrounded by people, but this was the boy that broke her heart. *Man*. This was the man who broke her heart. Now here he was, on her doorstep, looking far too fine. And they were alone. She could faintly hear the boys upstairs, and hoped that they wouldn't notice the visitor.

Kyle didn't seem surprised that she hadn't opened the door. He ducked his head for a moment, as if acknowledging that this must be awkward, then lifted it again, his mouth set in a straight line.

"Hey," he mouthed, then turned and pointed at the driveway.

She edged closer, peering out the side window. A green tractor was parked beside her Audi, a large farm wagon hitched behind it. She stared at the tractor, wondering if the next few minutes of her life could maybe not happen. When Kyle didn't magically disappear, she took a deep breath and opened the door.

"Hi."

"Your mom asked me to drive the wagon over."

She raised her eyebrows in disbelief. "My mom."

"Yeah. Laney ... I didn't know you were here, she didn't say."

She stared at him, words failing her. His returning gaze was warmer than she deserved for her rudeness, and she offered a weak smile.

"I was at Ted's place when she walked over. She said she wasn't dressed for riding a tractor."

"She was wearing jeans!"

Kyle shrugged. "I didn't think that much about it, I just drove the tractor across the road." He flicked his eyes over her and she pulled the blanket tighter. He took his time meeting her gaze again, and when he did, his smile was warm and interested. Was that wishful thinking on his part, or hers?

He raised his hand as if he might touch her arm, then changed his mind and waved instead as he stepped back. "I'll go now. It was nice to see you again."

She bit her lower lip as he turned and walked down the steps toward the gravel drive. He stepped past her car, and she realized he was departing on foot.

"Kyle?"

He turned in surprise and angled his head to the side in a silent response.

"Where are you going?"

"I just live down at the corner, in the old school house. I'm fixing it up. You should come by." And with that he turned and ambled down the drive, soon obscured by heavy oak branches. Laney stood in the doorframe watching for a few minutes, blanket wrapped around her shoulders, oblivious to the winter cold.

————

She didn't return to the couch until after dinner. Claire and Evie arrived home at the same time, and the afternoon swept by in a flurry of outdoor fun, indoor decorating and holiday baking. Laney didn't have a chance to talk to her mother about the meddling earlier, and as she sank into the soft cushions, wrapped once again in the afghan, she no longer felt the urgency. A day with Connor and Max was more exhausting than a 24-hour shift at the hospital.

Evie walked into the family room from the kitchen carrying two steaming mugs. "Chamomile tea? You look zonked."

Laney nodded and waved her hand at the coffee table. "Put it there, I'm too tired to even hold the cup right now. Your kids are full-on."

Evie giggled. "I know, right? They keep me on my toes."

"Mom putting them to bed?"

"Yep. She's a godsend."

"For you, maybe."

"What? Oh no, what did she do?"

Laney groaned, pushed herself into a sitting position, and reached for her tea. "She got Kyle to drive the tractor across the road today."

She expected shock or dismay, but Evie just pursed her lips.

"Come on, that was inappropriate."

Evie shook her head. "No, I get it. You've got stuff there you need to work through, and it's not happening if you pretend he doesn't exist."

Laney gaped at her sister. *Traitor.* "There's nothing to work through. He's an ex-boyfriend. It's awkward because it didn't end amicably. I've learned my lesson."

"Avoidance isn't resolution."

"It's been twelve years, our relationship is most definitely resolved."

"So you've moved on, healed your heart, fallen in love again?"

"Love is overrated." Laney willed herself to stay calm. "I've moved on and found satisfying relationships, yes."

"Really?"

"Absolutely."

"Tell me about your boyfriends."

Laney wrinkled her nose.

"See? You don't even like the word."

They were interrupted just then by footsteps coming down the stairs, but Laney didn't feel any relief. Evie on her own was one thing, but her sister and mother together would put on the full-court press. She thought of Kyle's invitation. Should she stop in and visit? She didn't agree that there was anything left to talk about, but she could acknowledge that it probably wasn't healthy to be tense about a college boyfriend more than a decade later.

"Anyone want some cookies?" Claire hovered in the doorway.

Laney kept her eyes trained on her lap, watching her fingers worry the loose knit of the afghan. She didn't want to catch her mother's eyes just yet, didn't want to invite her into a conversation Laney herself would prefer to get out of before it went any further. She didn't want to be rude, though, and snack prep would buy a few more minutes. "Mmmm. Yes, please. Thanks, Mom."

Evie waved their mother off and scooted to the edge of her seat, leaning toward Laney.

"You can't tell me that you want to be alone forever."

That pulled her up short. The last time she had used that word, she had been lying in Kyle's bed. The decade in between faded away and she stood in the tiny one-bedroom apartment in Windsor, watching her younger self unwind naked limbs from Kyle's lean frame.

"This is perfect. I'd like to stay in this moment forever."

"You could stay forever. You could marry me."

"You know I need to go to Harvard. It's just for a year."

"You could stay and do your master's degree here."

"And what if that's not enough? What if I don't get into medical school again? This is Harvard, Kyle. A once in a lifetime opportunity. I have to go."

"What about us?"

"You could come with me."

"I just got hired at the school board, you know I can't leave."

"Then I'll be home on holidays, and you can come visit me at March Break. You'll be able to concentrate on teaching, and then we'll be reunited for good next summer."

"And then you'll marry me."

"And then I'll marry you."

She hadn't told Evie that they were going to get married. Kyle had never officially proposed or given her a ring, and two weeks after that conversation, he abruptly broke up with her, telling Laney that a year apart was too much to ask. She had been devastated, and when it came time to apply to medical schools the following year, she only chose universities out of the province.

"Hey, where'd you go?" Evie waved a hand in front of Laney's face.

She blinked hard and shook her head. "Sorry, I'm more tired than I thought."

Her sister raised an eyebrow, but sat back in her chair and didn't say anything else until their mother brought in a plate of chewy ginger molasses cookies. "Mom, I was thinking that

I should take the boys into the city tomorrow to do a bit of last-minute shopping, do you want to come along?"

Claire looked at Laney and hesitated.

"Go with them, Mom. I'll catch up on some sleep. I have a bit of work to do too, I'll get that out of the way and then we'll have an entire week without any distractions."

Claire nodded and took a cookie. She might want to meddle, but for whatever reason she was giving that a pass tonight and Laney decided not to tempt fate. She gave her mom a tight squeeze, stole a cookie and plodded off to bed.

OTHER SERIES BY ZOE YORK

If you've enjoyed Wardham, you might want to visit **Pine Harbour** (small town military romance just a few hours north of Wardham), **Camp Firefly Falls** (sexy rom coms at an adult summer camp), as well as the Navy SEALs in **SEALs Undone** and **ASSIGNMENT: Caribbean Nights.**

And coming in 2017…the last book in the Wardham series, All That They Desire, which will segue into a brand-new series set in the same area, **Whisper Beach.** Wardham's getting even sexier!

Visit my website at zoeyork.com and join my mailing list to be the first to hear about new books!

ACKNOWLEDGEMENTS

AKA THE PEOPLE WHO MAKE ME SMILE IN A CRAZY BIG WAY

THIS book was written in a week and a half, and edited in about the same length of time, so not that many people knew about it. Those that did blew me away with their support. Those that didn't were thrilled when they heard about it after the fact. I'm grateful to and humbled by both groups.

Special notes of love and appreciation for:

My husband, who continues to smile and nod and love me unconditionally.

Molly, who read this first, in pieces, and told me when it was awesome and when it was not. Chapter Four is better because of her. Way better.

Bonnie and Ingrid, who turned on their retired teacher eyes (best eyes ever!) and hunted for typos.

Jennifer, who fixed an embarrassing number of tense slips and errant commas.

Mandie, Lori, Hannah, Rachel, Natalie and Andraena, who make it really easy to hit send on the email saying, "here's the latest book, what do you think?"

Book bloggers who embraced me as a totally unknown first time author and shared What Once Was Perfect: Nadine and Tamara from Hook Me Up Book Blog, Beth at Read Your Writes, Hootie and Globug from their eponymous blog (best nicknames ever!), Kim at Sugar and Spice Book Reviews, Eirene at Sleepless Nights Reviews, Caitlyn at Made For You Book Review, Savannah Mae, RomReader, Best Sellers and Best Stellars, and so many more.

Goodreads readers, who have friended me and welcomed me into their groups. Thank you, thank you, thank you. A particular note of appreciation for the "Some Like It Hot!" group, which continues to support me with honest early reviews, and provides awesome book chats when I need a break from writing.

Divas and Tweeters, who continue to push me to write as much and as well as I can in the spare hours I find in the day.

And finally, my readers. Holy crap, I have readers! I love each and every person who has read my book, joined my mailing list, written a review, tweeted or blogged or posted on Facebook...I can't thank you enough for your support. I love to hear from you, please keep the emails and messages coming!

ABOUT THE AUTHOR

Zoe York lives in London, Ontario with her young family. She's currently chugging Americanos, wiping sticky fingers, and dreaming of heroes in and out of uniform.

Connect with Zoe:
www.zoeyork.com
zoeyorkwrites@gmail.com

BE A WARDHAM AMBASSADOR

I'd love to have you join my Facebook reader group! Click on the link, or search "Wardham Ambassadors" on Facebook.